SUPERTATO

EVIL PEA RULES

For Lara, some editors are chosen for a very good reason.
Love from Sue and Paul

SIMON & SCHUSTER
First published in Great Britain in 2017
by Simon & Schuster UK Ltd
1st Floor, 222 Gray's Inn Road, London, WC1X 8HB
A CBS Company

A CIP catalogue record for this book is available
from the British Library upon request

978-1-4711-4406-6 (PB)
978-1-4711-4408-0 (eBook)

Printed in Italy

3 5 7 9 10 8 6 4 2

SUPERTATO

EVIL PEA RULES

by Sue Hendra and Paul Linnet

SIMON & SCHUSTER
London New York Sydney Toronto New Delhi

The Evil Pea sat upon his icy throne.
He was king of everything that he could see.

Unfortunately . . .

. . . all he could see was the inside of a boring old freezer! And he'd had enough of it.

It was night-time in the supermarket and all the good little veggies were settling down to sleep.

But this little veggie
wasn't sleepy at all.

'Hmmmmpfff!'
cried the cucumbers.

'Oh NO!' mouthed the melons. 'He's escaped!
The Evil Pea is back!'

'Of course I'm back!' shrieked the pea.
'Now how about a lovely haircut?'

Who could save these poor pineapples in peril?
Supertato, that's who!

'FREEZE!' he shouted.
'You're coming with me!'

And before the Evil Pea could get snippy . . .

... he was popped back
into the freezer
where he belonged.

The pea was furious.

'FREEZE, EH?
I'll give him FREEZE!

I'll give them ALL FREEZE!'

DANGER

And within seconds
he was out of the freezer
and up to no good.

Hrrrrrrr

The Evil Pea had a plan. It was his **craftiest** one yet.

With his pretend veggies in one hand and a freezy jet at the ready, he shouted in his best veggie voice . . .

SUPERTATO
TO THE . . . UH-OH!

'Take that!'
shouted the pea,
as he blasted Supertato
with the freezy jet!

'Time to chill out, Super**lolly**,' cackled the Evil Pea. 'What is it you always say? Some vegetables are frozen for a very good reason!

Mwa ha ha ha ha ha!'

And with that he zoomed off over aisles of sleeping veggies . . .

. . . to get ready for part two of his evil plan.

When the veggies woke up,
they couldn't believe their eyes.

Everywhere they looked, there was ice and snow.

'*Mwa ha ha ha ha!*' squealed the Evil Pea.

'How do you like the supermarket now, you nitwits?'

'WE LOVE IT!' cheered the veggies.

'NO!...NO!...NO!

It's not supposed to be FUN!'

Meanwhile our hero was still in a fix.
Luckily, the hot chillies had a plan.

'Quick everyone,
GROUP HUG!'

'Oooh, that should break the ice!'
said one pineapple to another.

And they were right!
Soon our hero was free . . .

And going on a – shopping spree?

'I'll be needing one of these . . .

one of these . . .

. . . and definitely one of these.'

'Ho-ho-hold it right there, Pea!' called Supertato.

'No sloping off for you.
We need to find out who's been
nice and who's been naughty . . .

. . . as if I didn't know.'

Everyone snuggled up on the sleigh.
'What a lovely tree,' said Supertato.
'There's just one thing missing . . .'

'Merry Christmas, Pea,' said Supertato.

'I know you're no angel.
But everyone's got to
start somewhere!'

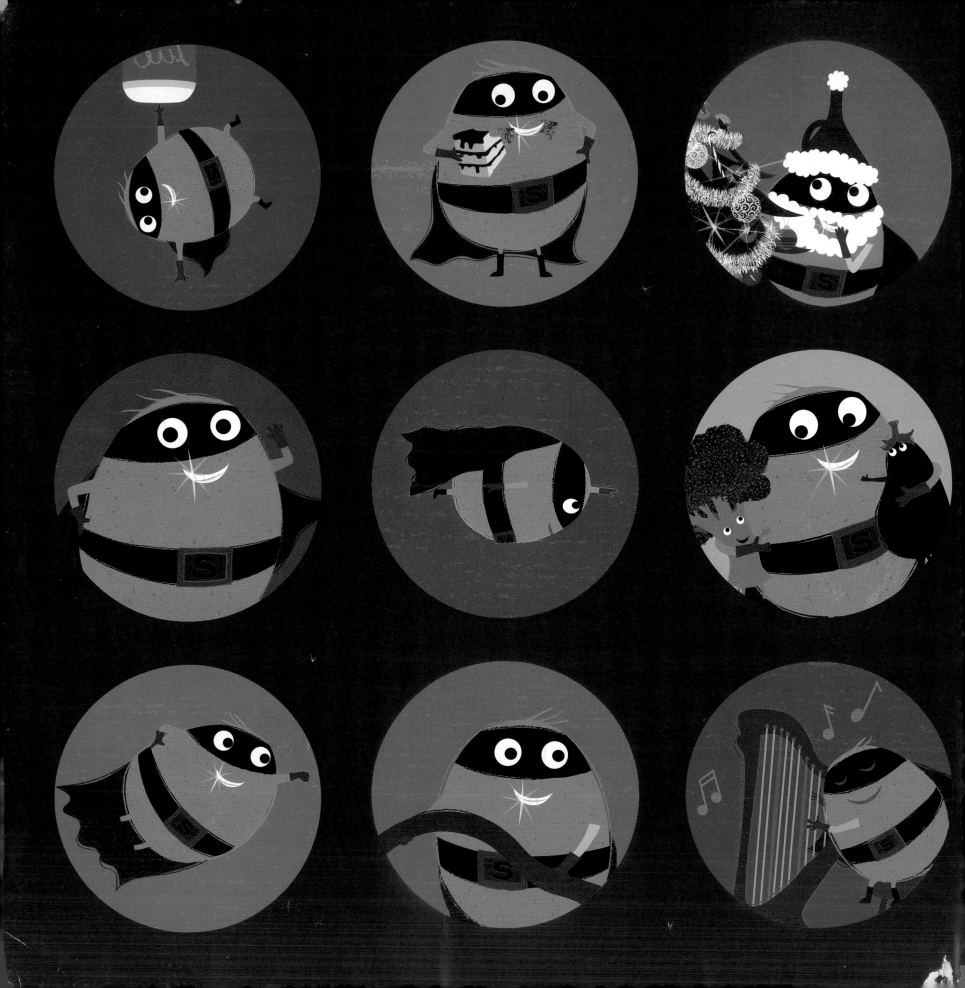

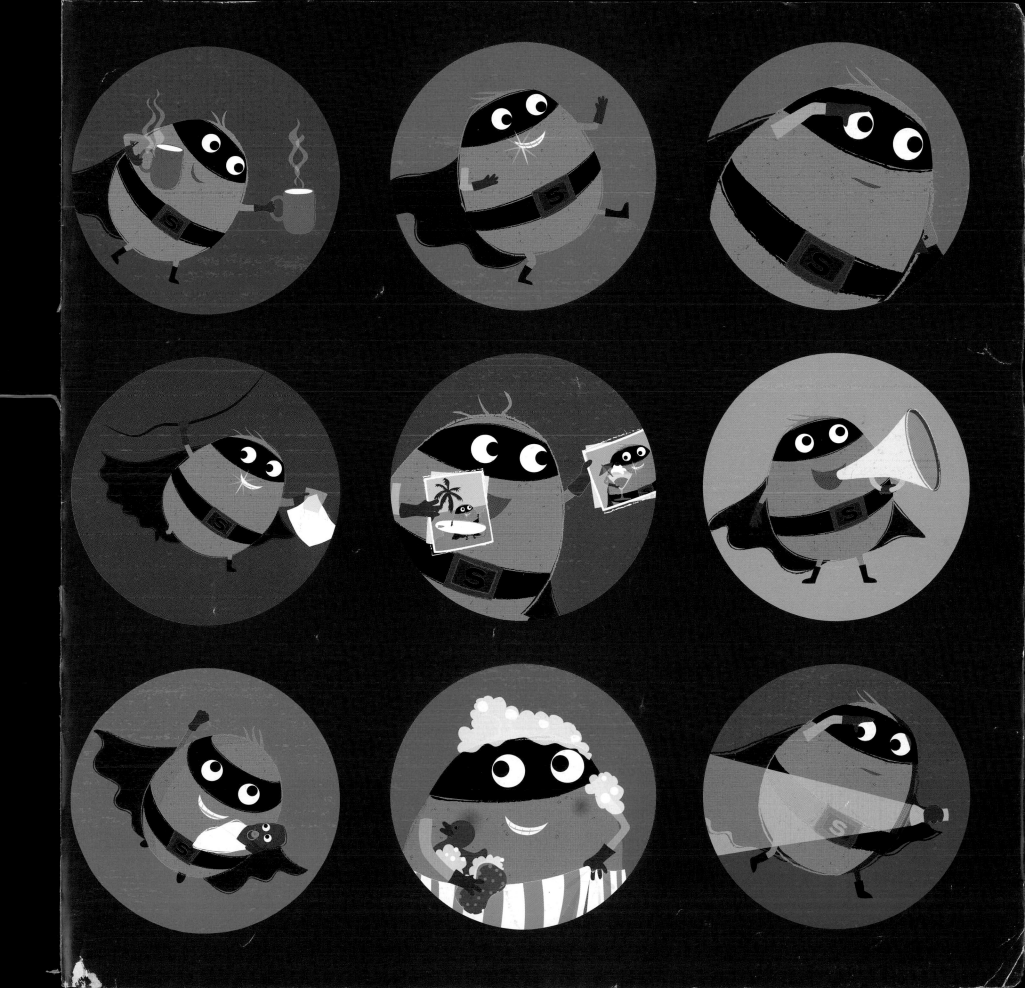